WHERE DID CAIN GET HIS WIFE?

SOME PEOPLE LIKE TO POINT TO THE STORY OF CAIN AND ABEL AS PROOF THE BIBLE IS INCORRECT.

THEY BASE THIS ON A MIS-UNDERSTANDING OF THE GENESIS ACCOUNT IN CHAPTER 4.

THE BIBLE RECORDS THE STORY OF TWO OF...

ONE SON WAS NAMED ABEL AND KEPT FLOCKS, WHILE THE OLDER SON'S NAME WAS CAIN AND HE WORKED THE SOIL.

GOD GAVE INSTRUCTION TO BOTH MEN ON HOW TO BRING AN OFFERING TO HIM.

GENESIS 4:1-16

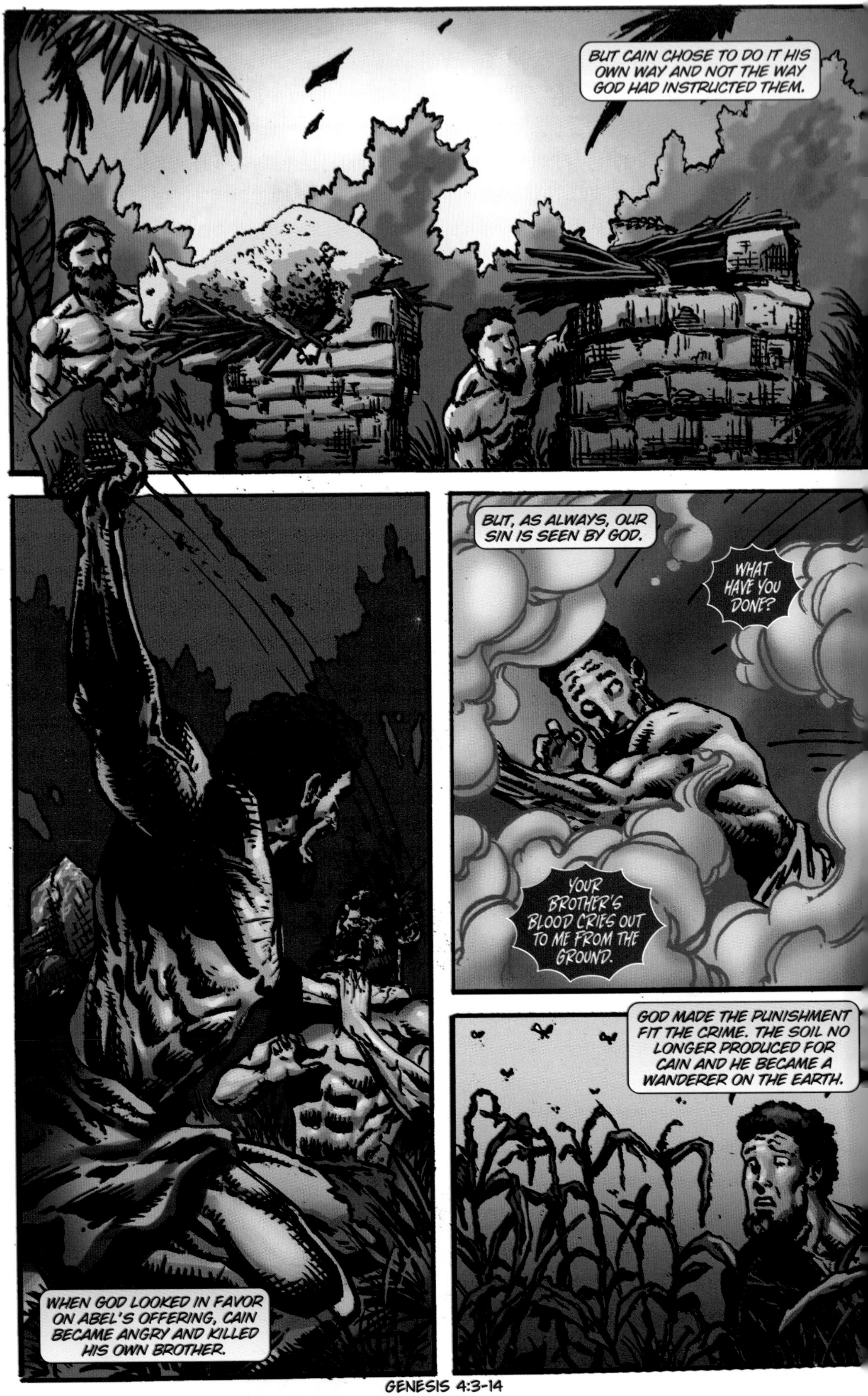
BUT CAIN CHOSE TO DO IT HIS OWN WAY AND NOT THE WAY GOD HAD INSTRUCTED THEM.
WHEN GOD LOOKED IN FAVOR ON ABEL'S OFFERING, CAIN BECAME ANGRY AND KILLED HIS OWN BROTHER.
BUT, AS ALWAYS, OUR SIN IS SEEN BY GOD.
WHAT HAVE YOU DONE?
YOUR BROTHER'S BLOOD CRIES OUT TO ME FROM THE GROUND.
GOD MADE THE PUNISHMENT FIT THE CRIME. THE SOIL NO LONGER PRODUCED FOR CAIN AND HE BECAME A WANDERER ON THE EARTH.

GENESIS 4:3-14

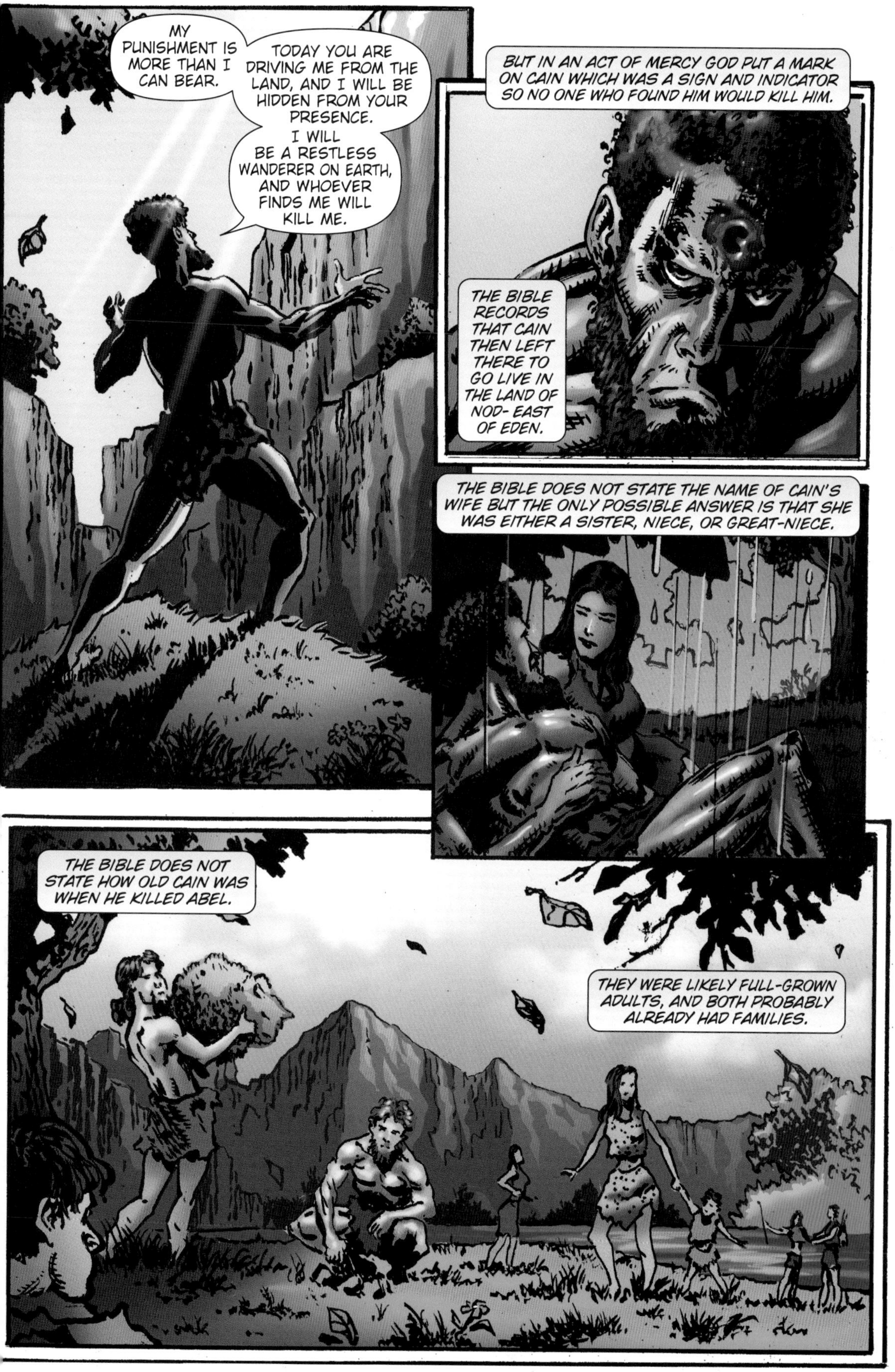
MY PUNISHMENT IS MORE THAN I CAN BEAR.
TODAY YOU ARE DRIVING ME FROM THE LAND, AND I WILL BE HIDDEN FROM YOUR PRESENCE.
I WILL BE A RESTLESS WANDERER ON EARTH, AND WHOEVER FINDS ME WILL KILL ME.
BUT IN AN ACT OF MERCY GOD PUT A MARK ON CAIN WHICH WAS A SIGN AND INDICATOR SO NO ONE WHO FOUND HIM WOULD KILL HIM.
THE BIBLE RECORDS THAT CAIN THEN LEFT THERE TO GO LIVE IN THE LAND OF NOD- EAST OF EDEN.
THE BIBLE DOES NOT STATE THE NAME OF CAIN'S WIFE BUT THE ONLY POSSIBLE ANSWER IS THAT SHE WAS EITHER A SISTER, NIECE, OR GREAT-NIECE.
THE BIBLE DOES NOT STATE HOW OLD CAIN WAS WHEN HE KILLED ABEL.
THEY WERE LIKELY FULL-GROWN ADULTS, AND BOTH PROBABLY ALREADY HAD FAMILIES.

ADAM AND EVE WERE THE FIRST (AND ONLY) HUMAN BEINGS, SO THEIR CHILDREN WOULD HAVE NO CHOICE BUT TO INTERMARRY.

TODAY, WHEN TWO PEOPLE WHO ARE RELATED TO EACH OTHER AND HAVE SIMILAR GENETICS HAVE CHILDREN TOGETHER--

-- THERE IS A HIGH RISK OF RECESSIVE CHARACTERISTICS BECOMING DOMINANT AND GENETIC ABNORMALITIES CAN OCCUR.

WHEN PEOPLE COME FROM DIFFERENT FAMILIES OR "BLOODLINES" THEN IT IS HIGHLY UNLIKELY THAT BOTH PARENTS WILL CARRY THE SAME RECESSIVE TRAIT.

BUT ADAM AND EVE, AS THE ORIGINAL MAN AND WOMAN CREATED BY GOD, DID NOT HAVE ANY GENETIC DEFECTS--

-- WHICH ALLOWED THE FIRST GENERATIONS OF THEIR DESCENDANTS TO HAVE A CLEAN GENE POOL.

MUCH LATER ON GOD DIRECTED MOSES TO FORBID INTER-FAMILY MARRIAGE AFTER THERE WERE ENOUGH PEOPLE TO MAKE INTERMARRIAGE UNNECESSARY.

GENESIS 1:27, LEVITICUS 18:6-18

WE DON'T KNOW HOW MANY SONS AND DAUGHTERS ADAM AND EVE HAD— OR THE FULL NUMBER THEIR OFFSPRING HAD.

BY THE TIME OF ABEL'S MURDER THE MEN COULD HAVE BEEN 40 OR THEY COULD HAVE BEEN 100, WITH MANY GENERATIONS IN BETWEEN.

THE FACT THAT CAIN WAS SCARED FOR HIS LIFE INDICATES THAT THERE WERE LIKELY MANY CHILDREN AND GRANDCHILDREN LIVING AT THE TIME.

CAIN WAS RIGHTLY SCARED THAT ONE OF THE OTHERS WOULD REVENGE ABEL'S KILLING.

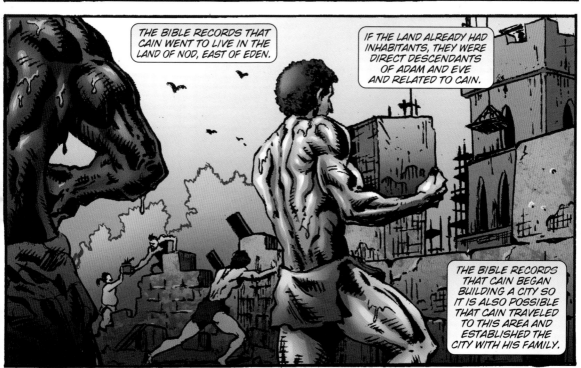

THE BIBLE RECORDS THAT CAIN WENT TO LIVE IN THE LAND OF NOD, EAST OF EDEN.

IF THE LAND ALREADY HAD INHABITANTS, THEY WERE DIRECT DESCENDANTS OF ADAM AND EVE AND RELATED TO CAIN.

THE BIBLE RECORDS THAT CAIN BEGAN BUILDING A CITY SO IT IS ALSO POSSIBLE THAT CAIN TRAVELED TO THIS AREA AND ESTABLISHED THE CITY WITH HIS FAMILY.

GENESIS 4:16-17

WHAT DOES THE BIBLE SAY ABOUT DINOSAURS?

DINOSAURS ARE A PART OF A LARGER DEBATE OVER ORIGINS, THE AGE OF THE EARTH--

-- AND INTERPRETING THE EVIDENCES WE HAVE.

DINOSAURS WERE POPULARIZED WHEN IN 1822 MARY ANNE MANTELL OF SUSSEX, ENGLAND FOUND A STONE GLITTERING IN THE SUNLIGHT AND SHOWED IT TO HER FOSSIL-HUNTING HUSBAND.

IN 1841 SIR RICHARD OWEN, THE FIRST SUPERINTENDENT OF THE BRITISH MUSEUM, COINED THE TERM *DINOSAUR*- FROM THE GREEK WORDS MEANING "TERRIBLE LIZARD."

ALL SCIENTISTS HAVE THE SAME FACTS AND THE SAME FOSSILS.

SOME APPROACH THE ISSUE OF DINOSAURS FROM AN EVOLUTIONARY STANDPOINT, AND OTHERS FROM THE STANDPOINT THAT THE BIBLE IS A WRITTEN REVELATION FROM GOD AND AN ACCURATE DESCRIPTION OF HISTORY.

THOSE WHO HOLD TO AN OLDER VIEW OF THE EARTH DO NOT THINK THE BIBLE MENTIONS DINOASURS AND BELIEVE THAT DINOSAURS EVOLVED 235 MILLION YEARS AGO, BEFORE MAN.

THEY THEORIZE THAT AROUND 65 MILLION YEARS AGO A CATACLYSMIC EVENT KILLED THE DINOSAURS, THOUGH THEY ARE NOT IN AGREEMENT ON WHAT THAT EVENT WAS.

SINCE THE WORD 'DINOSAUR' WAS NOT EVEN INVENTED UNTIL 1841 IT IS NOT USED IN THE BIBLE.

Dinosaur

THE TANNIYN APPEARS TO HAVE BEEN SOME SORT OF GIANT REPTILE. THESE CREATURES ARE MENTIONED NEARLY THIRTY TIMES IN THE OLD TESTAMENT AND WERE FOUND BOTH ON LAND AND IN THE WATER

THE OLD TESTAMENT USES THE HEBREW WORD TANNIYN, WHICH IS TRANSLATED "SEA MONSTER," AND SOMETIMES AS "SERPENT." BUT IT IS MOST COMMONLY TRANSLATED "DRAGON."

THE BIBLE TEACHES THAT GOD MADE THE DINOSAURS, AS WELL AS OTHER LAND ANIMALS ON DAY FIVE OF CREATION.

ADAM AND EVE WERE CREATED ON DAY SIX, SO DINOSAURS LIVED AT THE SAME TIME AS HUMANS--

-- NOT SEPARATED BY EONS OF AGES AS COMMONLY TAUGHT.

FROM THE BIBLE WE SEE THAT THERE WAS NO DEATH, BLOOD-SHED OR SUFFERING BEFORE SIN ENTERED THE WORLD.

DEATH AND BLOOD-SHED CAME INTO THE WORLD ONLY AFTER ADAM AND EVE SINNED.

THIS WAS ALSO A PICTURE OF THE ATONEMENT--

-- FORESHADOWING CHRIST'S BLOOD THAT WAS TO BE SHED FOR US.

THE FIRST DEATH OF AN ANIMAL OCCURRED WHEN GOD SHED AN ANIMAL'S BLOOD IN THE GARDEN OF EDEN AND CLOTHED ADAM AND EVE.

DINOSAURS COULD NOT HAVE DIED OUT BEFORE PEOPLE APPEARED BECAUSE DINOSAURS HAD NOT PREVIOUSLY EXISTED; AND DEATH, BLOODSHED, DISEASE AND SUFFERING ARE A RESULT OF ADAM'S SIN.

DEAD ANIMALS BEFORE SIN WOULD CONTRADICT AND UNDERMINE THE GOSPEL OF CHRIST.

GENESIS 3:21, GENESIS 1:29-30, ROMANS 5:12, 14, 1 CORINTHIANS 15:21-22

REPRESENTATIVES OF ALL KINDS OF AIR-BREATHING LAND ANIMALS WENT ON BOARD THE ARK WITH NOAH AS DESCRIBED BY THE BIBLE--

-- INCLUDING JUVENILE DINOSAURS.

THE ANIMALS OUTSIDE THE ARK PERISHED IN THE CATACLYSMIC FLOOD AND THEIR REMAINS BECAME THE FOSSILS WE VIEW TODAY.

AFTER THE FLOOD THE ANIMALS CAME OFF THE ARK BUT IT WAS A MUCH DIFFERENT WORLD THAN BEFORE THE FLOOD.

POST-FLOOD CLIMACTIC CHANGE, LACK OF FOOD, DISEASE, AND MAN'S HUNTING CAUSED MANY TYPES OF ANIMALS TO BECOME EXTINCT.

APPROXIMATELY 800 MAMMALS, REPTILES, AMPHIBIANS, BIRDS, FISHES, INVERTEBRATES AND PLANTS BECAME EXTINCT BETWEEN 1500-2000.

BLACK RHINOCEROS

DODO BIRD

GOLDEN TOAD

NEARLY A THIRD OF THE WORLD'S AMPHIBIAN SPECIES HAVE BECOME EXTINCT SINCE 1980.

THE DINOSAURS, LIKE MANY OTHER CREATURES, SIMPLY BECAME EXTINCT OVER TIME, THOUGH WE HAVE MANY LIVING FOSSILS ALIVE EVEN TODAY.

SCIENTISTS ACCEPT THE MAMMOTH DRAWINGS IN CAVES, SO IT SHOULD SEEM REASONABLE TO ALSO ACCEPT OTHER DEPICTIONS OF MEN WITH DINOSAURS.

THERE ARE ALSO MANY EXTRA-BIBLICAL ACCOUNTS OF DINOSAURS AND MAN CO-EXISTING.

NEARLY EVERY ANCIENT CIVILIZATION HAS SOME SORT OF ART DEPICTING GIANT REPTILIAN CREATURES.

NORTH AMERICA HAS PETROGLYPHS, ARTIFACTS, AND CLAY FIGURINES OF DINOSAURS.

ROCK CARVINGS IN SOUTH AMERICA DEPICT MEN RIDING DIPLODOCUS-LIKE CREATURES AND ALSO IMAGES OF TRICERATOPS-LIKE, PTERODACTYL-LIKE, AND TYRANNOSAURUS REX-LIKE CREATURES.

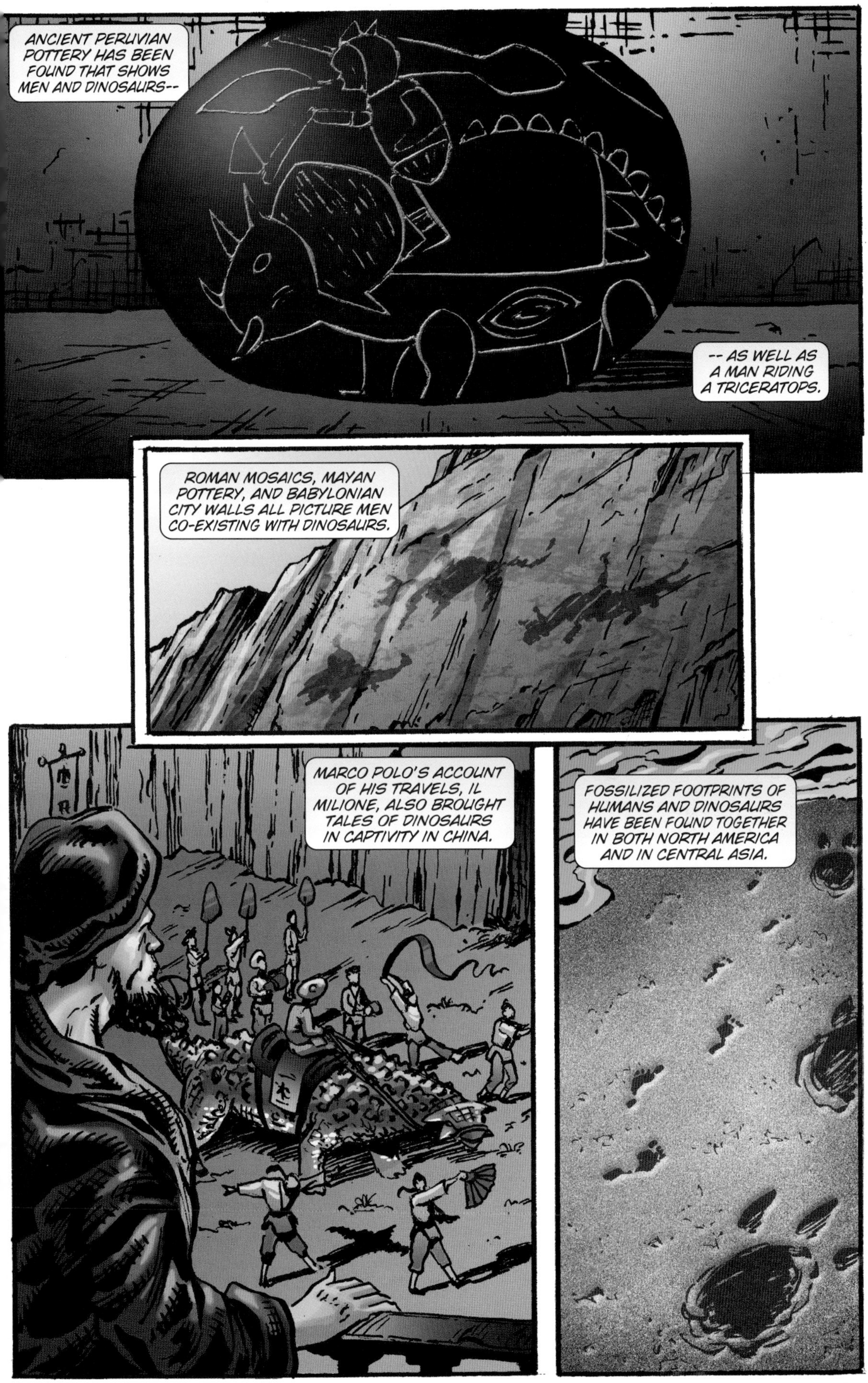

ANCIENT PERUVIAN POTTERY HAS BEEN FOUND THAT SHOWS MEN AND DINOSAURS--
-- AS WELL AS A MAN RIDING A TRICERATOPS.
ROMAN MOSAICS, MAYAN POTTERY, AND BABYLONIAN CITY WALLS ALL PICTURE MEN CO-EXISTING WITH DINOSAURS.
MARCO POLO'S ACCOUNT OF HIS TRAVELS, IL MILIONE, ALSO BROUGHT TALES OF DINOSAURS IN CAPTIVITY IN CHINA.
FOSSILIZED FOOTPRINTS OF HUMANS AND DINOSAURS HAVE BEEN FOUND TOGETHER IN BOTH NORTH AMERICA AND IN CENTRAL ASIA.

A SUMERIAN EPIC OF AROUND 2000 BC TELLS OF GILGAMESH'S ENCOUNTER WITH A VICIOUS DRAGON THAT HE KILLED AND DECAPITATED.

WHEN ALEXANDER THE GREAT MARCHED INTO INDIA IN 330 BC THEY FOUND THE INDIANS WORSHIPPING HUGE HISSING REPTILES THEY KEPT IN CAVES.

ENGLAND AND OTHER CULTURES PRESERVE THE STORY OF ST. GEORGE WHO SLEW A DRAGON.

IN THE 1500'S, A EUROPEAN SCIENTIFIC BOOK, HISTORIA ANIMALIUM, LISTED SEVERAL LIVING ANIMALS THAT WE WOULD CALL DINOSAURS.

A WELL-KNOWN NATURALIST OF THE TIME, ULYSSES ALDROVANDUS, RECORDED AN ENCOUNTER BETWEEN A PEASANT NAMED BAPTISTA AND A DRAGON WHOSE DESCRIPTION FITS THAT OF THE SMALL DINOSAUR TANYSTROPHEUS.

THE ENCOUNTER WAS ON MAY 13, 1572, NEAR BOLOGNA, ITALY, AND THE PEASANT KILLED THE DRAGON.

IF WE CAN'T BELIEVE THE BIBLE ABOUT HISTORY, HOW CAN WE TRUST ITS MORAL ASPECTS AND ITS MESSAGE OF SALVATION?

IF THE EVOLUTIONISTS' TEACHING OF MILLIONS OF YEARS OF DINOSAURS WITH DEATH AND SUFFERING IS TRUE, THEN THE BIBLICAL ACCOUNT IS FALSE.

IF THE BIBLE IS WRONG IN THIS AREA- THEN HOW CAN WE TRUST IT IN OTHER AREAS?

IF EVERYTHING IN CREATION JUST MADE ITSELF THROUGH NATURAL PROCESSES, THEN THERE WAS NO SPECIAL CREATION.

IF GOD DID NOT MAKE US THEN HE WOULD HAVE NO RIGHT TO TELL US HOW TO LIVE.

WITHOUT MORALITY THERE IS NO SIN. IF THERE IS NO SIN, THEN THERE IS NO NEED FOR A SAVIOR.

THE BIBLE'S DEPICTION OF DINOSAURS IS ACCURATE AND GOD'S REVELATION OF ANCIENT HISTORY CAN BE TRUSTED.

BIBLICAL TEACHING OF ORIGINS IS KEY FOR PEOPLE TO UNDERSTAND GOD'S PUNISHMENT OF SIN AND OUR NEED FOR HIS SAVIOR, JESUS CHRIST, SENT TO SAVE HUMANS FROM SIN.

WHERE WAS JESUS FOR THE THREE DAYS BETWEEN HIS DEATH AND RESURRECTION?

THERE IS CONFUSION ABOUT WHAT HAPPENED AFTER CHRIST'S DEATH ON THE CROSS. PART OF THIS CONFUSION COMES FROM THE APOSTLE'S CREED, "HE DESCENDED INTO HELL."

IN THE HEBREW SCRIPTURES THE WORD USED TO DESCRIBE THE PLACE OF THE DEAD IS SHEOL.

THE GREEK WORD FOR IT IS "HADES" WHICH IS ALSO "THE PLACE OF THE DEAD."

SHEOL HAD TWO DIVISIONS— THE ABODE OF THE RIGHTEOUS DEAD AND THE ABODE OF THE UNRIGHTEOUS DEAD. THE ABODE OF THE RIGHTEOUS DEAD WAS CALLED "PARADISE" AND "ABRAHAM'S BOSOM."

LUKE 16:26

THESE TWO ABODES ARE SEPARATED BY A "GREAT CHASM."

HELL (THE LAKE OF FIRE) IS THE PERMANENT AND FINAL PLACE OF JUDGMENT FOR THE LOST.

HADES IS A TEMPORARY PLACE. SO JESUS DID NOT GO TO HELL AS HELL IS A FUTURE REALM, ONLY PUT INTO EFFECT AFTER THE GREAT WHITE THRONE JUDGMENT.

IT SEEMS THAT BETWEEN HIS DEATH AND RESURRECTION CHRIST VISITED THE TEMPORARY REALM OF THE DEAD WHERE HE DELIVERED A MESSAGE TO SPIRIT BEINGS.

THIS IS NOT PREACHING IN THE USUAL NEW TESTAMENT SENSE OF PREACHING THE GOSPEL, BUT RATHER THE HERALDING OF A MESSAGE.

IT WAS NOT A MESSAGE OF REDEMPTION SINCE ANGELS CANNOT BE SAVED.

JESUS WAS NOT GIVING PEOPLE A SECOND CHANCE FOR SALVATION AS THE BIBLE SAYS WE FACE JUDGMENT AFTER DEATH, NOT A SECOND CHANCE.

REVELATION 20:11-15, I PETER 3:19, HEBREWS 2;16, HEBREWS 9:27

I PETER 3:22, COLOSSIANS 2:15, LUKE 16:20, LUKE 16:23, LUKE 16:43, EPHESIANS 4:8-10

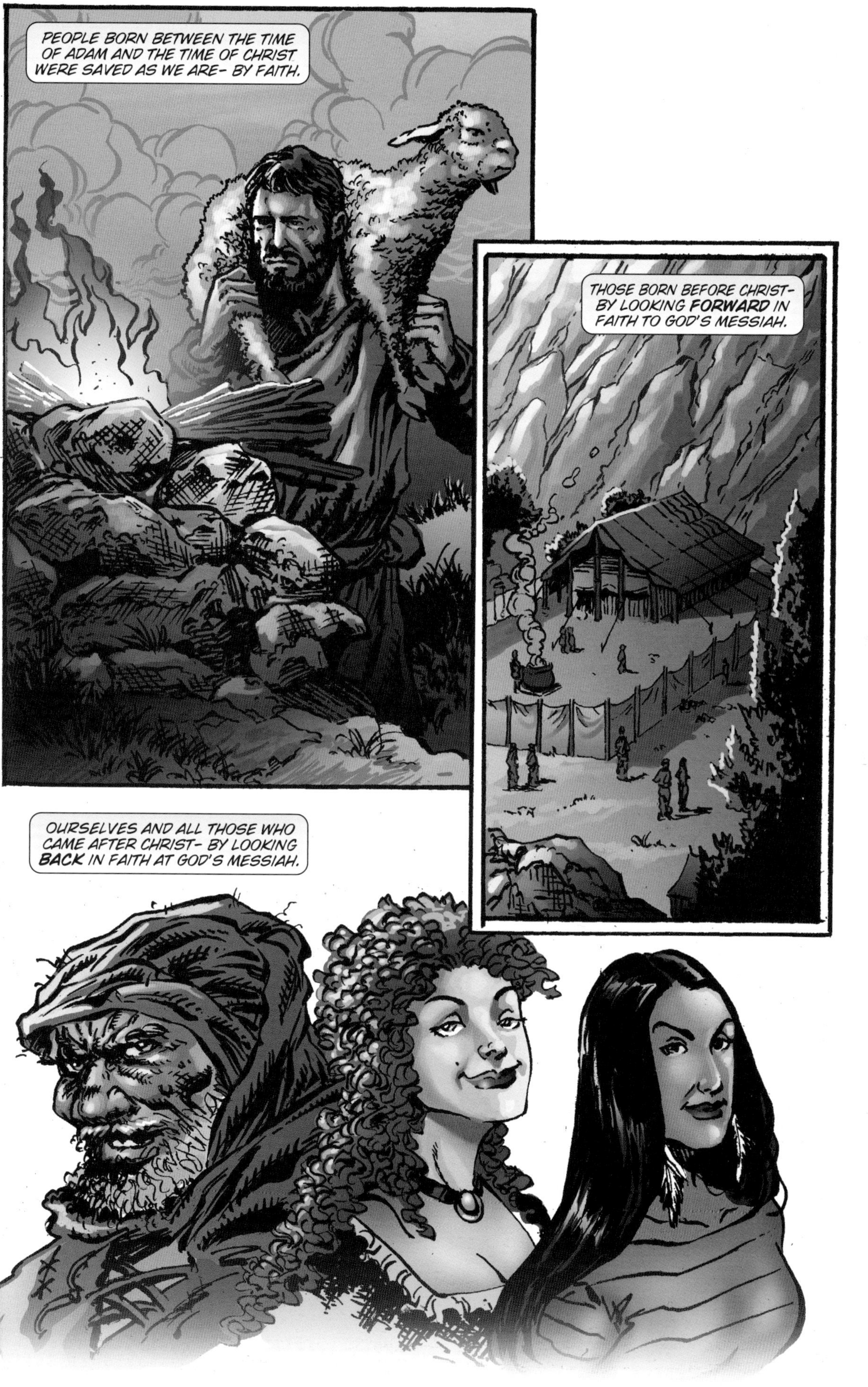
PEOPLE BORN BETWEEN THE TIME OF ADAM AND THE TIME OF CHRIST WERE SAVED AS WE ARE- BY FAITH.
THOSE BORN BEFORE CHRIST- BY LOOKING FORWARD IN FAITH TO GOD'S MESSIAH.
OURSELVES AND ALL THOSE WHO CAME AFTER CHRIST- BY LOOKING BACK IN FAITH AT GOD'S MESSIAH.

WHAT HAPPENS TO PEOPLE RIGHT AFTER DEATH?

THERE ARE A LOT OF DIFFERENT OPINIONS ABOUT WHAT HAPPENS TO SOMEONE WHEN THEY DIE.

SOME PEOPLE THINK THERE IS 'SOUL SLEEP' WHERE YOUR SOUL "SLEEPS" UNTIL A FUTURE RESURRECTION.

SOME RELIGIONS TEACH REINCARNATION- THAT OUR SOUL OR SPIRIT COMES BACK IN A DIFFERENT FORM.

OTHERS TEACH ANNIHILATION- THAT A PERSON JUST SIMPLY CEASES TO EXIST.

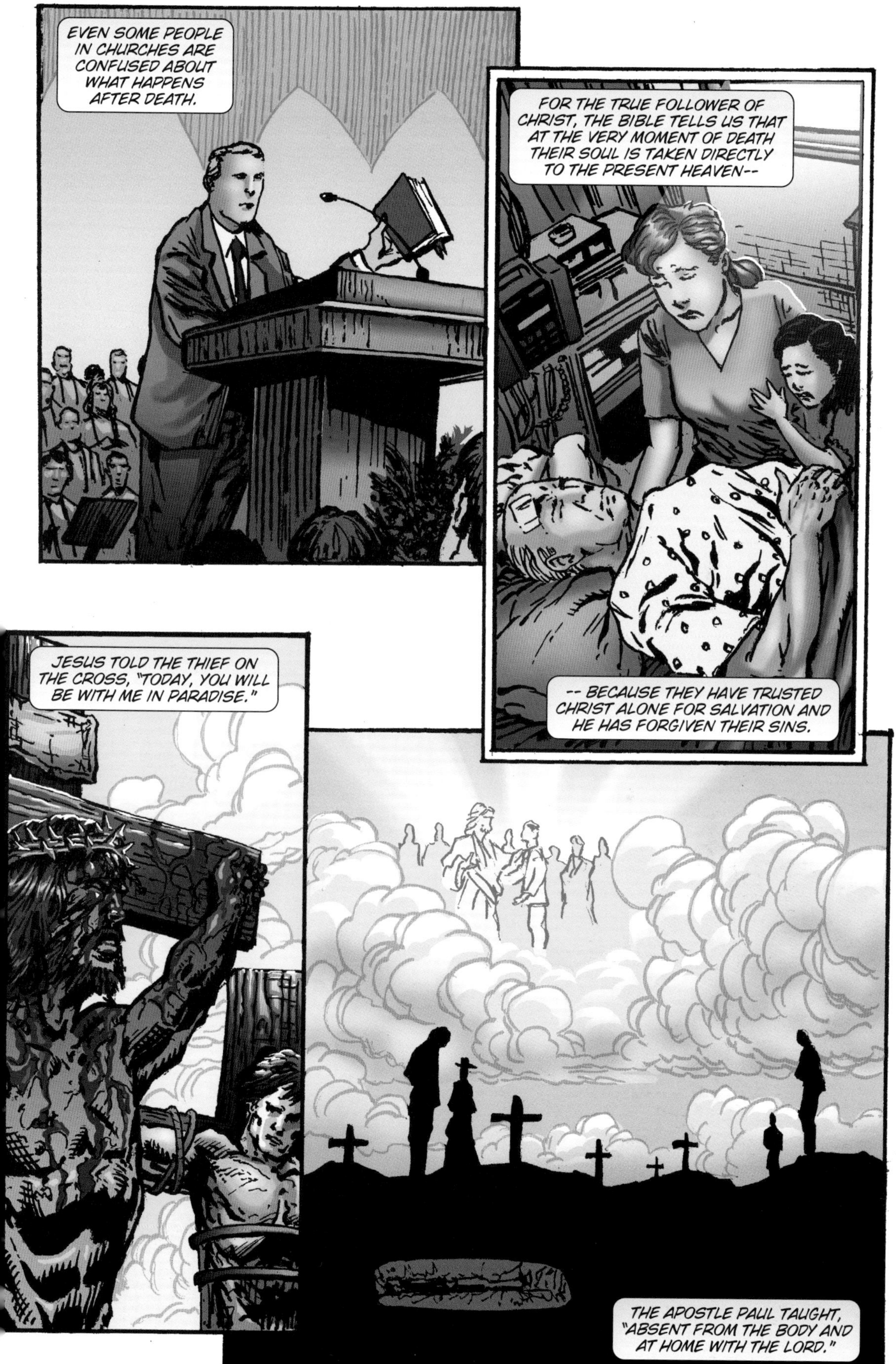
EVEN SOME PEOPLE IN CHURCHES ARE CONFUSED ABOUT WHAT HAPPENS AFTER DEATH.
FOR THE TRUE FOLLOWER OF CHRIST, THE BIBLE TELLS US THAT AT THE VERY MOMENT OF DEATH THEIR SOUL IS TAKEN DIRECTLY TO THE PRESENT HEAVEN--
-- BECAUSE THEY HAVE TRUSTED CHRIST ALONE FOR SALVATION AND HE HAS FORGIVEN THEIR SINS.
JESUS TOLD THE THIEF ON THE CROSS, "TODAY, YOU WILL BE WITH ME IN PARADISE."
THE APOSTLE PAUL TAUGHT, "ABSENT FROM THE BODY AND AT HOME WITH THE LORD."

2 CORINTHIANS 5:6-8

WHILE THE SOULS OR SPIRITS OF BELIEVERS GO TO BE WITH CHRIST IMMEDIATELY AFTER DEATH, THE PHYSICAL BODY REMAINS IN THE GRAVE "SLEEPING."

AFTER DEATH ALL PEOPLE RESIDE IN A "TEMPORARY" HEAVEN OR HELL.

LIKELY, PEOPLE WILL HAVE A TEMPORARY BODY DURING THIS TIME BEFORE THE SPIRIT IS REUNITED WITH THEIR RESURRECTED BODY.

JOHN 5:29

THE BIBLE TEACHES THAT AT THE RESURRECTION BODY AND SOUL WILL BE REUNITED.

BUT THE DESTINY PEOPLE CHOSE BEFORE DEATH WILL NOT CHANGE.

SOME WILL RISE TO THE RESURRECTION OF THE JUST.

SOME TO THE RESURRECTION OF DAMNATION.

JOHN 5:29

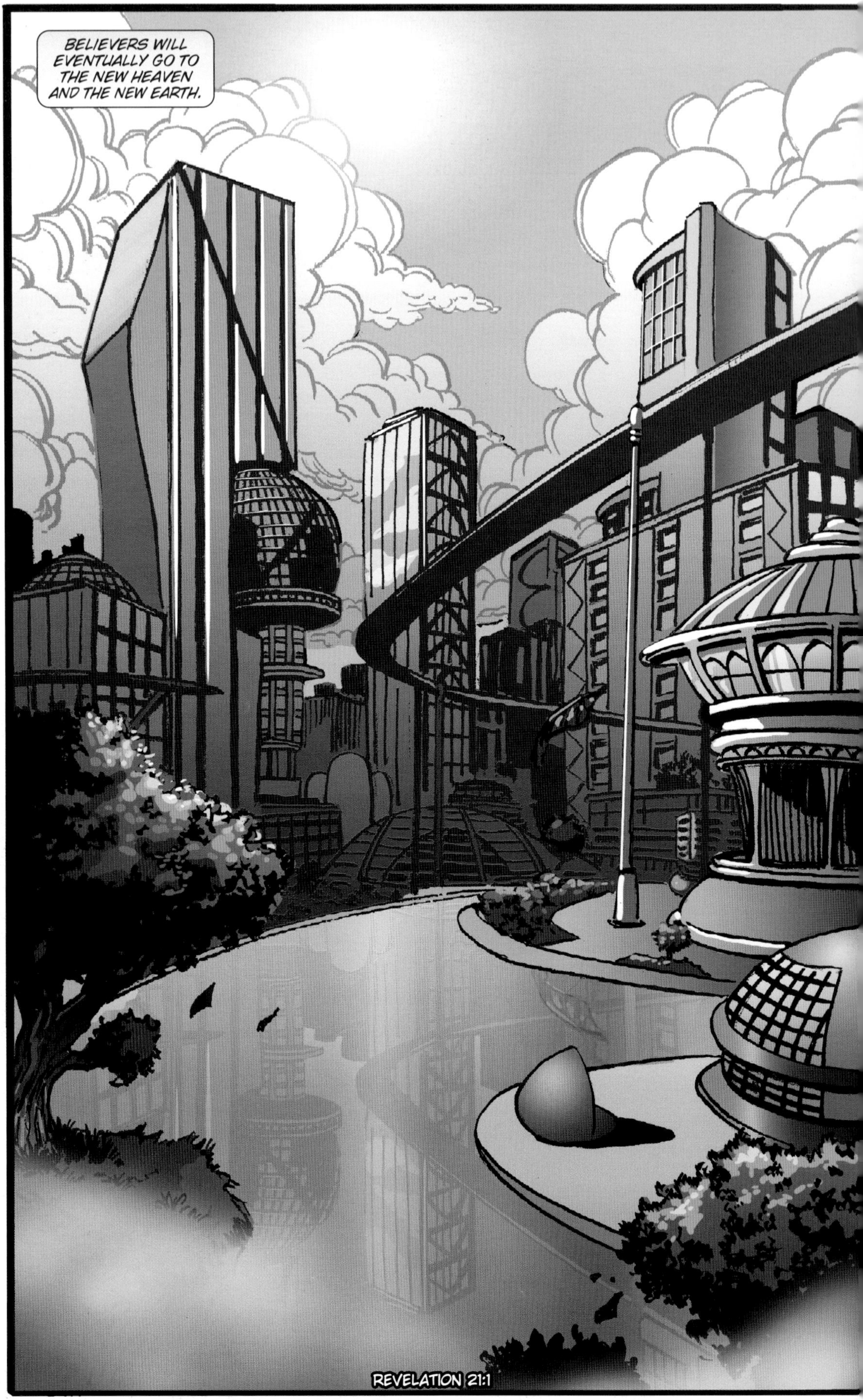
BELIEVERS WILL EVENTUALLY GO TO THE NEW HEAVEN AND THE NEW EARTH.
REVELATION 21:1

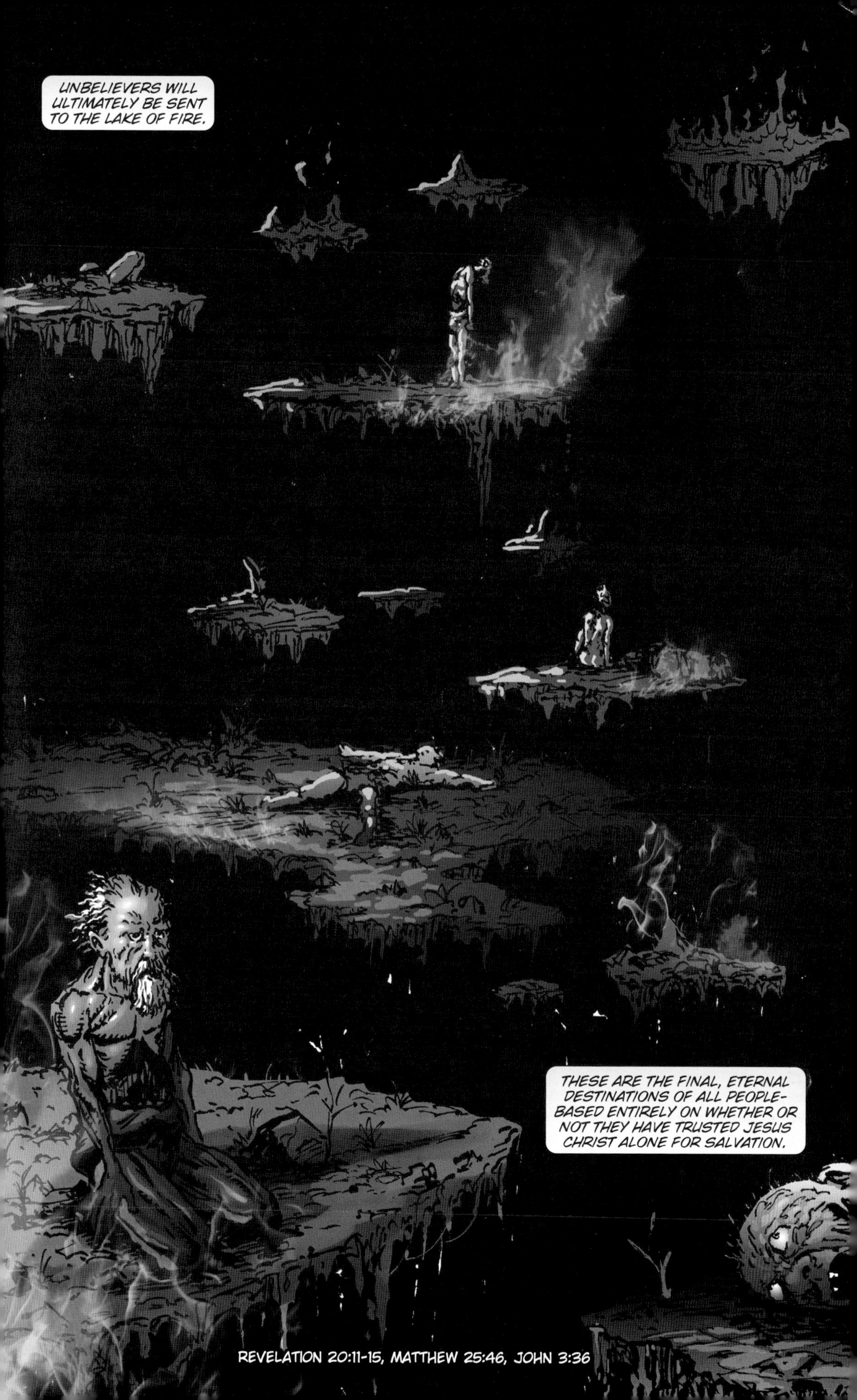
UNBELIEVERS WILL ULTIMATELY BE SENT TO THE LAKE OF FIRE.
THESE ARE THE FINAL, ETERNAL DESTINATIONS OF ALL PEOPLE- BASED ENTIRELY ON WHETHER OR NOT THEY HAVE TRUSTED JESUS CHRIST ALONE FOR SALVATION.
REVELATION 20:11-15, MATTHEW 25:46, JOHN 3:36

ARE THERE SUCH THINGS AS ALIENS OR UFOS?

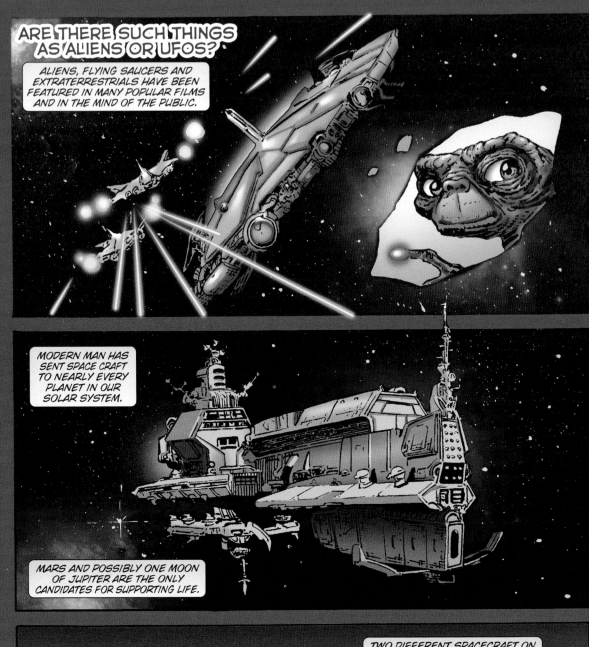

ALIENS, FLYING SAUCERS AND EXTRATERRESTRIALS HAVE BEEN FEATURED IN MANY POPULAR FILMS AND IN THE MIND OF THE PUBLIC.

MODERN MAN HAS SENT SPACE CRAFT TO NEARLY EVERY PLANET IN OUR SOLAR SYSTEM.

MARS AND POSSIBLY ONE MOON OF JUPITER ARE THE ONLY CANDIDATES FOR SUPPORTING LIFE.

TWO DIFFERENT SPACECRAFT ON MARS- INCLUDING PATHFINDER- TOOK MANY SAMPLES AND CONDUCTED MANY EXPERIMENTS.

THEY FOUND ABSOLUTELY NO SIGN OF LIFE.

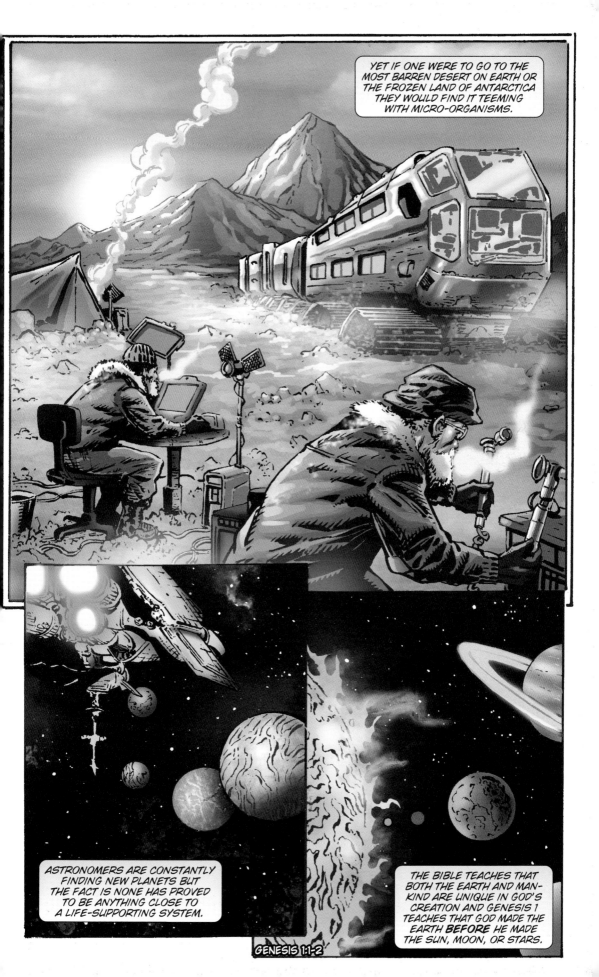

YET IF ONE WERE TO GO TO THE MOST BARREN DESERT ON EARTH OR THE FROZEN LAND OF ANTARCTICA THEY WOULD FIND IT TEEMING WITH MICRO-ORGANISMS.

ASTRONOMERS ARE CONSTANTLY FINDING NEW PLANETS BUT THE FACT IS NONE HAS PROVED TO BE ANYTHING CLOSE TO A LIFE-SUPPORTING SYSTEM.

THE BIBLE TEACHES THAT BOTH THE EARTH AND MAN-KIND ARE UNIQUE IN GOD'S CREATION AND GENESIS 1 TEACHES THAT GOD MADE THE EARTH **BEFORE** HE MADE THE SUN, MOON, OR STARS.

GENESIS 1:1-2

THE BIBLE ALSO TELLS US THAT AFTER THE FIRST MAN AND WOMAN SINNED- SICKNESS AND DEATH ENTERED THE WORLD.

IF ALL OF CREATION SUFFERS UNDER THE CURSE OF SIN, THEN IT WOULD ALSO HOLD THAT ANY LIFE APART FROM EARTH WOULD ALSO SUFFER.

PEOPLE WHO BELIEVE IN EVOLUTION WANT VERY BADLY TO FIND ANOTHER PLANET IN ANOTHER SOLAR SYSTEM TO SUPPORT THE NOTION THAT LIFE MUST HAVE EVOLVED.

Seti Project

BUT SCRIPTURE TEACHES THAT GOD MADE FROM ONE MAN EVERY NATION OF MANKIND TO LIVE ON ALL THE FACE OF THE EARTH- AS WELL AS DETERMINED THEIR ALLOTTED YEARS AND THE BOUNDARIES OF THEIR DWELLING PLACE.

HIS HOPE IS THAT PEOPLE WOULD SEEK HIM, IN THE HOPE THAT THEY MIGHT FEEL THEIR WAY TOWARD HIM AND FIND HIM.

ACTS 17:26-27

THERE IS NO REASON TO ATTRIBUTE UNEXPLAINED PHENOMENA TO ALIENS OR UFOS.

IF THERE IS A CAUSE TO THESE SUPPOSED EVENTS, IT IS LIKELY TO BE DEMONIC IN ORIGIN.

THE BIBLE, WHICH IS A WRITTEN REVELATION FROM GOD, TELLS NOTHING OF ALIENS IN THE CREATION ACCOUNT AND THEY ARE NOT MENTIONED ANYWHERE ELSE IN THE SCRIPTURES.

THE FALLEN ANGEL, SATAN, AND THE OTHER FALLEN ANGELS HAVE HAD AS THEIR DESIRE SINCE THE BEGINNING--

BUT THE BIBLE DOES TELL OF VISITORS FROM ANOTHER WORLD- INSTANCES OF DEMONS (FALLEN ANGELS) VISITING THE EARTH HAVE BEEN WITNESSED AND RECORDED.

-- TO DRAW HUMANITY AWAY FROM THE WORSHIP OF GOD AND TO TURN MANKIND'S ATTENTION TOWARDS THEMSELVES.

GENESIS 6 DESCRIBES THESE VISITATIONS, AND THE OLDEST KNOWN CULTURE– THE SUMERIANS– DESCRIBED "ANUNNAKI"–

YOU SHALL BE LIKE GOD.

– DEITIES THAT CAME FROM HEAVEN TO DWELL ON EARTH WITH MEN, OFTEN IN THE FORM OF SNAKES.

FROM EVE'S EXPERIENCE, WE CAN SEE THAT DEMONS USE THE TEMPTATION OF SUPERIOR WISDOM TO ENSNARE MEN AND THAT WE ARE VERY SUSCEPTIBLE TO THAT.

FOR THIS REASON IT IS ENTIRELY PLAUSIBLE THAT "ALIENS" COULD BE PART OF AN END TIMES DECEPTION OF MANKIND.

THE BIBLE SAYS THAT PEOPLE WILL NOT BELIEVE THE TRUTH...

... BUT THEY WILL BELIEVE A LIE.

APE MAN

EARLY STAGE *

GENESIS 6:1-4, MATTHEW 24:24, II THESSALONIANS 2:9-11

THE BIBLE ALSO FORETELLS THE COMING OF "THE LAW-LESS ONE THAT WILL BE IN ACCORDANCE WITH SIGNS AND WONDERS" THAT SERVE THE LIE.

THE BIBLE TELLS US THAT THE WORLD WILL UNITE UNDER THE POWER OF THIS MAN CALLED THE ANTICHRIST.

SINCE THE ANTICHRIST WILL UNITE ALL WORLD RELIGIONS IT IS POSSIBLE THAT HE (POSSESSED BY A DEMON) COULD CLAIM TO HAVE HIGHER EVOLUTIONARY DEVELOPMENT.

OR HE COULD CLAIM TO BE ONE SENT BY ALIENS TO SAVE AND UNITE THE WORLD.

SATAN IS A MASTER OF DECEPTION SO THERE ARE A NUMBER OF PLAUSIBLE OPTIONS SURROUNDING THE ANTICHRIST THAT INCLUDE "ALIENS."

REVELATION 13:1-10

SCIENTISTS AND EXPERTS COULD PROCLAIM THAT A 'HIGHLY EVOLVED' CREATURE WAS VISITING WITH 'DIVINE' NEWS TO SAVE THE EARTH.

THIS DECEPTION COULD ALSO INCLUDE AN "EXTRA-TERRESTRIAL" EXPLANATION FOR LIFE ON EARTH, WORLD RELIGIONS AND MIRACULOUS SIGNS, AND COULD BE VERY PERSUASIVE IN DECEIVING PEOPLE WHO DO KNOW OR UNDERSTAND THE BIBLE.

ALL OF THESE LIES AND SIGNS COULD BE VERY INFLUENTIAL IN DECEIVING LARGE NUMBERS OF PEOPLE WHO DO NOT KNOW OR UNDERSTAND THE BIBLE.

IN FACT THE BIBLE TELLS US THAT BECAUSE PEOPLE WILL REFUSE TO LOVE THE TRUTH AND BE SAVED, THAT GOD SENDS THEM A POWERFUL DELUSION SO THAT THEY WILL BELIEVE A LIE.

THE BIBLE IS STILL THE MOST TRUSTWORTHY SOURCE ON ALL THINGS EXTRATERRESTRIAL.

II THESSALONIANS 2:9-11; 2 TIMOTHY 3:16

WHAT DOES THE BIBLE SAY ABOUT ANGELS?

WHEN GOD CREATED THE WORLD THERE WERE DIFFERENT ORDERS OF CREATION.

ANIMALS WERE ONE CREATED ORDER. MANKIND WAS ANOTHER.

BUT BEFORE BOTH OF THESE- GOD CREATED A SPECIAL ORDER CALLED ANGELS.

GENESIS 1:1 - 2:25; EZEKIEL 28:12-15

ANGELS ARE CREATED BEINGS THAT HAVE INTELLIGENCE, EMOTIONS, AND WILLS.

BUT BECAUSE THEY ARE CREATED, THEIR KNOWLEDGE IS LIMITED.

LIKE ALL CREATED BEINGS, THEY ARE SUBJECT TO THE WILL OF GOD.

MATTHEW 8:29; 2 CORINTHIANS 11:3; 1 PETER 1:12; LUKE 2:13; JAMES 2:19; REVELATION 12:17; LUKE 8:28-31

PSALM 148:1-2; ISAIAH 6:3; HEBREWS 1:6; REVELATION 5:8-13; JOB 38:6-7; PSALM 103:20; REVELATION 22:9

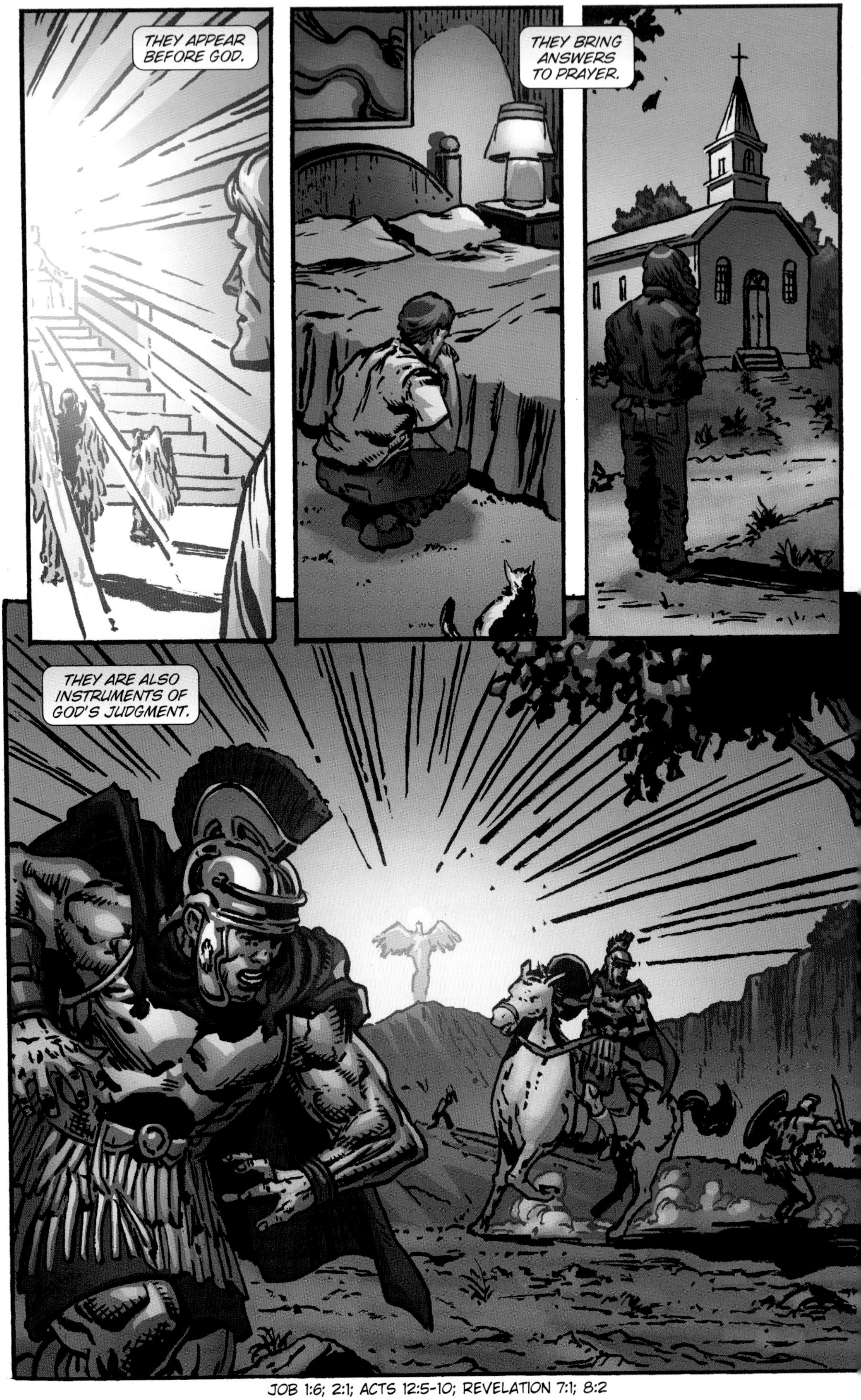
THEY APPEAR BEFORE GOD.
THEY BRING ANSWERS TO PRAYER.
THEY ARE ALSO INSTRUMENTS OF GOD'S JUDGMENT.

JOB 1:6; 2:1; ACTS 12:5-10; REVELATION 7:1; 8:2

ACTS 8:26; 10:3; 1 CORINTHIANS 4:9; 11:10; EPHESIANS 3:10; 1 PETER 1:12

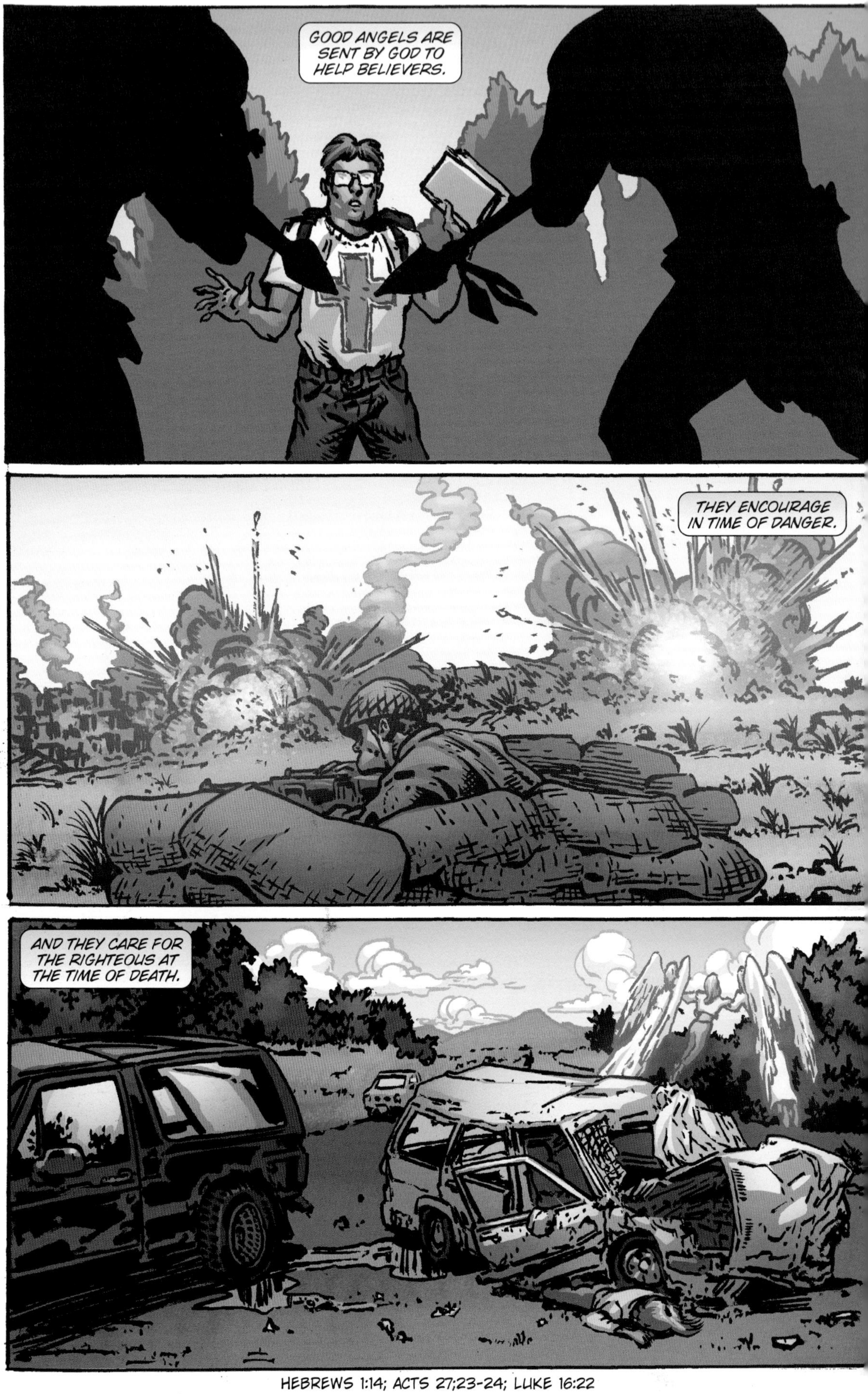
GOOD ANGELS ARE SENT BY GOD TO HELP BELIEVERS.
THEY ENCOURAGE IN TIME OF DANGER.
AND THEY CARE FOR THE RIGHTEOUS AT THE TIME OF DEATH.

HEBREWS 1:14; ACTS 27;23-24; LUKE 16:22

THEY DO SEEM TO HAVE GREATER KNOWLEDGE THAN HUMANS, WHICH MAY BE FOR THREE REASONS.

FIRST, ANGELS WERE CREATED AS AN ORDER OF CREATURES HIGHER THAN HUMANS.

SECOND, ANGELS KNOW THE BIBLE AND STUDY THE WORLD MORE THOROUGHLY THAN HUMANS DO AND GAIN KNOWLEDGE FROM IT.

THIRD, ANGELS HAVE EXPERIENCED THE PAST AND THEY HAVE GAINED KNOWLEDGE THROUGH LONG OBSERVATION OF HUMAN ACTIVITIES.

EZEKIEL 28:12-14; JAMES 2:19; REVELATION 12:12

SOME PEOPLE MISTAKENLY BELIEVE THAT PEOPLE BECOME ANGELS WHEN THEY DIE.

BUT THE BIBLE TEACHES THAT ANGELS ARE AN ENTIRELY DIFFERENT CREATED ORDER OF BEINGS THAN HUMANS.

HUMAN BEINGS DO NOT BECOME ANGELS AFTER THEY DIE.

ANGELS WILL NEVER BECOME, AND NEVER WERE, HUMAN BEINGS.

ANGELS ARE SPIRITUAL BEINGS THAT CAN, TO A CERTAIN DEGREE, TAKE ON PHYSICAL FORM.

HUMANS ARE PRIMARILY PHYSICAL BEINGS, BUT WITH A SPIRITUAL ASPECT.

ONE OF THE GREATEST THINGS WE CAN LEARN FROM THE HOLY ANGELS IS THEIR INSTANT, UNQUESTIONING OBEDIENCE TO GOD'S COMMANDS.

GENESIS 1:26; HEBREWS 1:14

WHAT DOES THE BIBLE SAY ABOUT DEMONS?

JUST AS THERE ARE GOOD SPIRITUAL BEINGS CALLED ANGELS THAT DO GOD'S WILL- THERE IS ANOTHER CLASS OF SPIRITUAL BEINGS WHO ARE FALLEN ANGELS. THESE ARE CALLED DEMONS.

ANGELS WERE CREATED BY GOD BEFORE THE CREATION OF THE EARTH.

AT ONE TIME SATAN WAS ONE OF GOD'S CHIEF ANGELS- MAYBE EVEN THE TOP ANGEL.

HE WAS UNSURPASSED IN BRILLIANCE AND INTELLIGENCE.

HE HELPED LEAD IN WORSHIP OF GOD.

HE WAS ONE OF THE TOP ANGELS- AN ARCHANGEL.

JOB 38:4-7; ISAIAH 14:12-15; EZEKIEL 28:12-15

WE DON'T KNOW EXACTLY WHAT HAPPENED BUT THE BIBLE SAYS THAT SATAN HAD PRIDE IN HIS HEART AND SAID HE WANTED TO BE LIKE GOD.

SATAN DIDN'T WANT TO JUST LOOK AT GOD'S THRONE- HE WANTED TO BE ON IT- HE WANTED TO BE GOD.

INTERESTINGLY- THIS IS THE SAME TEMPTATION AND LIE HE USED IN THE GARDEN WITH ADAM AND EVE- AND USES EVEN TODAY- HE TELLS PEOPLE THEY CAN BE LIKE GOD.

THE FALL OF LUCIFER AND THE REBELLION OF ANGELS WHO FOLLOWED HIM HAPPENED SOMETIME AFTER THEY WERE CREATED AND BEFORE THE CREATION OF MAN.

ISAIAH 14:12-15; EZEKIEL 28:12-15

THAT DAY SATAN LED A REBELLION IN HEAVEN AND THE BIBLE INDICATES THAT A THIRD OF THE ANGELS JOINED HIM.

WE DON'T KNOW HOW MANY ANGELS THERE WERE EXCEPT THE BIBLE STATES THOUSANDS UPON THOUSANDS WHICH WOULD INDICATE IN THE MILLIONS AT LEAST.

WHEN THE REBELLION OCCURRED GOD AND HIS HOLY ANGELS BANISHED THESE FALLEN ANGELS FROM HEAVEN AND THEY WERE CAST TO EARTH.

ISAIAH 14:12-15; EZEKIEL 28:12-15; REVELATION 12:4

HEY, WHY DON'T YOU SKIP THE YOUTH GROUP AND COME CHECK OUT THE PARTY.

SOME BIBLICAL SCHOLARS FEEL MOST OF THE FOUR GOSPELS ARE REALLY NOT THE WORDS OF JESUS BUT RATHER...

BIBLE SEMINAR

SATAN AND HIS DEMONS NOW LOOK TO DESTROY AND DECEIVE ALL THOSE WHO FOLLOW AND WORSHIP GOD.

THEY SEEK TO SPREAD FALSE TEACHING AS WELL AS TO DECEIVE THE WORLD.

MORONI WAS THE LAST PROPHET AND RETURNED TO EARTH AS AN ANGEL IN 1827 TO REVEAL THIS BOOK TO JOSEPH SMITH...

THEY SEEK TO TURN PEOPLE AWAY FROM BELIEVING THE BIBLE IS TRUE AND THAT SALVATION IS FOUND IN JESUS CHRIST ALONE.

I PETER 5:8; II CORINTHIANS 11:14-15; II CORINTHIANS 4:4

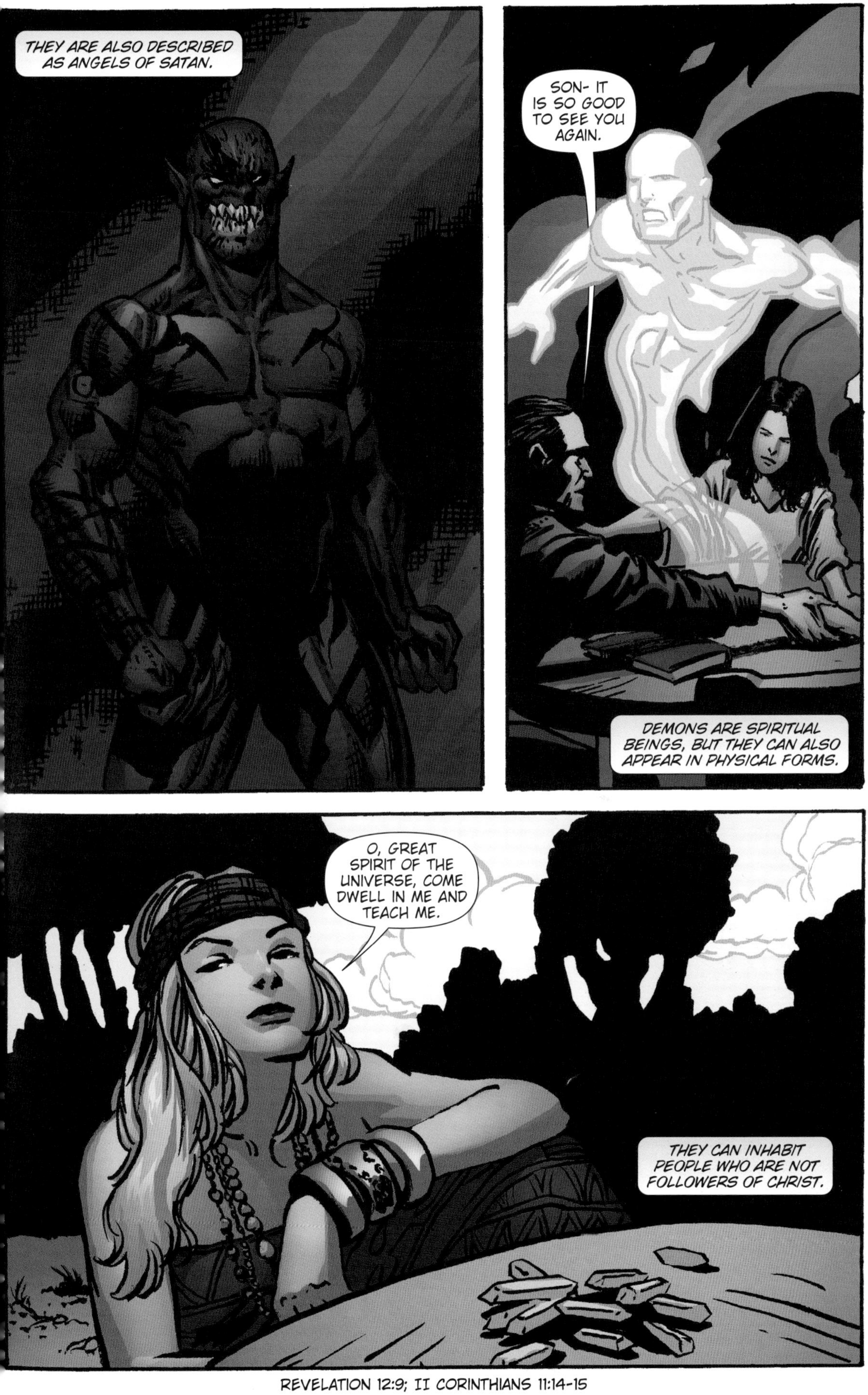
THEY ARE ALSO DESCRIBED AS ANGELS OF SATAN.
SON- IT IS SO GOOD TO SEE YOU AGAIN.
DEMONS ARE SPIRITUAL BEINGS, BUT THEY CAN ALSO APPEAR IN PHYSICAL FORMS.
O, GREAT SPIRIT OF THE UNIVERSE, COME DWELL IN ME AND TEACH ME.
THEY CAN INHABIT PEOPLE WHO ARE NOT FOLLOWERS OF CHRIST.

REVELATION 12:9; II CORINTHIANS 11:14-15

II CORINTHIANS 12:7; I PETER 5:8; REVELATION 12:4-9; MATTHEW 4:1-11

PEOPLE WHO SEEK TO FIND GOD'S WILL IN OUIJA BOARDS, HOROSCOPES, CRYSTALS, DRUGS, CARDS, MAGIC AND THE OCCULT ARE NOT MEETING THE CHRISTIAN GOD.

INSTEAD, THEY ARE IN THE REALM WHERE FALLEN ANGELS WORK AND DECEIVE PEOPLE.

THERE SEEMS TO BE A HEIRARCHICAL STRUCTURE RANGING FROM CHIEF DEMONS TO DEMONS WITH LESSER POWERS.

THAT IS WHY PRAYER, FASTING (GOING WITHOUT FOOD), OBEDIENCE, AND MEMORIZING SCRIPTURE ARE CONSIDERED WEAPONS FOR BELIEVERS TO USE IN WHAT THE BIBLE CALLS A **SPIRITUAL BATTLE**.

EPHESIANS 6:12; DANIEL 10:13

IN THE BIBLE THESE FALLEN ANGELS ARE ALSO CALLED UNCLEAN OR EVIL SPIRITS.

HOWEVER, EVERY TIME THEY WERE CONFRONTED BY JESUS THEY HAD TO LEAVE.

LET ME GO WITH YOU.

GO HOME TO YOUR FRIENDS AND TELL THEM HOW MUCH THE LORD HAS DONE FOR YOU, AND HOW HE HAS HAD MERCY ON YOU.

THE DEMONS/FALLEN ANGELS ARE ENEMIES OF GOD- BUT THEY ARE DEFEATED ENEMIES.

JUST AS THERE WAS A LOT OF DEMONIC ACTIVITY WHILE JESUS CHRIST WAS ON EARTH WE CAN LIKELY EXPECT INCREASED DEMONIC ACTIVITY AS THE TIME NEARS FOR CHRIST TO RETURN.

JESUS PROMISED HIS FOLLOWERS COMPLETE AUTHORITY AND POWER OVER FALLEN ANGELS.

SO WHEN MOVIES COME ALONG ABOUT DEMON POSSESSION WE DO NOT HAVE ANYTHING TO FEAR.

JESUS- NOT RELIGION- HAS TOTAL AUTHORITY OVER ALL DEMONS AND OVER ALL DARK FORCES.

MARK 10:1; MARK 5:1-20; I JOHN 4:4

WILL ANIMALS AND OUR PETS BE IN HEAVEN?

THE BIBLE TALKS A LOT ABOUT ANIMALS AND GOD GIVES GREAT SIGNIFICANCE TO ANIMALS AS EARTH'S SECOND MOST VALUABLE INHABITANTS.

OUR RELATIONSHIPS WITH ANIMALS ARE AN IMPORTANT PART OF OUR LIVES AND WE HAVE A GOD-GIVEN AFFECTION FOR ANIMALS.

THE PROPHET ISAIAH SPOKE OF A TIME COMING ON EARTH WHEN ANIMALS WOULD CO-EXIST PEACEFULLY.

THE WOLF AND THE LAMB WILL LIE DOWN TOGETHER... THEY WILL NEITHER HARM NOR DESTROY ON ALL MY HOLY MOUNTAIN.

THE SCRIPTURES TEACH THAT WHAT WAS LOST IN THE GARDEN- GOD WILL RESTORE IN THE NEW EARTH.

ISAIAH 11:6-9; ISAIAH 65:17, 66:2; 65:25

THROUGHOUT THE SCRIPTURES GOD USES ANIMALS TO ACCOMPLISH HIS PURPOSES–

A PROPHET BEING FED BY RAVENS, A DONKEY CARRYING JESUS, A FISH TO SWALLOW JONAH–

AND A DONKEY TO GET BALAAM'S ATTENTION.

IN MANY PLACES THE BIBLE RELATES GOD'S CONCERN FOR ANIMALS.

IN THE STORY OF JONAH ONE OF THE THINGS GOD SAYS TO JONAH, BESIDES HIS CONCERN FOR THE PEOPLE, WAS ALSO HIS CONCERN OVER THE CATTLE.

GOD'S CARE FOR ANIMALS IS EVEN SEEN IN THE TEN COMMANDMENTS WHERE HE ALSO WANTED THE ANIMALS TO HAVE SABBATH RESTS.

GOD CREATED US TO BE STEWARDS OF ANIMALS AND NOT MIS TREAT THEM

AND IN BOTH THE PSALMS AND THE LAST BOOK OF THE BIBLE, THE REVELATION, WE ARE TOLD HOW ANIMALS ALSO PRAISE GOD.

JONAH 4:11; DEUTERONOMY 5:14; PROVERBS 12:10; REVELATION 5:13

IN THE BOOK OF ROMANS THE APOSTLE PAUL INDICATES THAT GOD'S INVISIBLE QUALITIES AND HIS DIVINE ATTRIBUTES ARE SEEN IN CREATION.

THIS INCLUDES NOT ONLY THE HEAVENLY BODIES AND NATURE- BUT ANIMALS AS WELL.

WHEN ADAM WAS CREATED- GOD SURROUNDED HIM WITH ANIMALS.

WHEN NOAH WAS DELIVERED-

GOD SURROUNDED HIM WITH ANIMALS.

WHEN JESUS WAS BORN- GOD SURROUNDED HIM WITH ANIMALS.

AS EVIDENCED BY THE MANY SCRIPTURES, GOD CARES ABOUT ANIMALS AND HAS A FUTURE PLAN FOR THEM.

WHAT GOD BEGAN WE CAN EXPECT HIM TO FINISH WELL.

IN THE GARDEN OF EDEN IT WAS PARADISE LOST, BUT IN THE NEW EARTH IT WILL BE PARADISE RESTORED.

ROMANS 1:20; GENESIS 2:19-20; GENESIS 7:14-16; LUKE 2:7

WHEN GOD BREATHED A SPIRIT INTO ADAM'S BODY, MADE FROM THE EARTH, HE BECAME A NEPHESH- OR LIVING BEING.

THE HEBREW WORD NEPHESH IS A "LIVING BEING" OR "SOUL."

ANIMALS, LIKE HUMANS, WERE FORMED FROM THE GROUND.

THE SAME WORD- NEPHESH- IS USED FOR ANIMALS- WHO ALSO HAVE "THE BREATH OF LIFE" IN THEM.

WHEN GOD MADE THE ANIMALS HE SAID THAT "IT WAS GOOD."

MAN DID NOT EVOLVE FROM ANIMALS BUT WAS CREATED SEPARATELY FROM ANIMALS.

MAN WAS CREATED IN GOD'S IMAGE- WITH A CONSCIENCE- AND LIKE HIM MORALLY, RATIONALLY, EMOTIONALLY AND SOCIALLY.

MAN'S BODY WAS PERFECT, A REFLECTION OF GOD'S HOLINESS.

HE WAS CREATED LAST- AND WAS GOD'S "FINISHING TOUCH."

BUT BOTH HUMANS AND ANIMALS HAVE THIS IN COMMON- THEY ARE LIVING BEINGS- OR NEPHESH- CREATED BY A CREATOR.

GENESIS 2:7; GENESIS 2:19: GENESIS 1:25

BUT WHEN ADAM AND EVE SINNED AND SIN CAME INTO THE WORLD- ANIMALS ALSO SUFFERED AS A PART OF THE CURSE OF SIN ON MANKIND AND THE WORLD.

THE BIBLE RECORDS THAT AFTER MANY GENERATIONS MANKIND BECAME SO CORRUPT AND VIOLENT THAT GOD TOLD NOAH HE WAS GOING TO WIPE OUT MANKIND AND START OVER.

ANIMALS, INCLUDING DINOSAURS, WERE A PART OF GOD'S ORIGINAL CREATION. THE LAND ANIMALS NOT IN THE ARK DIED IN THE FLOOD.

BUT WHEN GOD SAVED PEOPLE FROM THE DESTRUCTION OF THE FLOOD HE ALSO TOOK CARE TO SAVE ANIMALS- THE PEOPLE'S COMPANIONS AND HELPERS.

WHEN GOD MADE THE COVENANT WITH NOAH, HE SAID HE WAS MAKING IT WITH HIM AND WITH EVERY LIVING CREATURE THAT WAS WITH HIM.

GENESIS 6:11-13; GENESIS 9:9-17; GENESIS 6:19-20; GENESIS 9:8-11

IF GOD'S PLAN FOR EARTH AFTER THE FLOOD INCLUDED ANIMALS- IT IS MOST LIKELY THAT GOD'S PLAN FOR A NEW EARTH ALSO INCLUDES ANIMALS.

THE BIBLE STATES THAT GOD'S FIRST JUDGMENT WAS BY WATER (THE FLOOD) BUT HIS FINAL JUDGMENT ON THE EARTH WILL BE BY FIRE.

IF THE RESCUE OF ANIMALS WAS A PART OF THE FIRST JUDGMENT WE ALSO SHOULD ANTICIPATE THAT GOD'S RESCUE AND RESTORATION OF ANIMALS WILL HAPPEN AFTER THE SECOND JUDGMENT.

CHRIST DID NOT DIE FOR ANIMALS THE WAY HE DIED FOR THE SIN OF MANKIND BUT HE DID DIE INDIRECTLY FOR ANIMALS IN THAT ALL CREATION (INCLUDING ANIMALS) WILL BE REDEEMED.

IN SPEAKING OF THE IMPACT AND FAR-REACHING SCOPE OF CHRIST'S RESURRECTION, AND GOD'S REDEMPTION OF THE WORLD, THE APOSTLE PAUL WROTE THIS...

THE CREATION ITSELF WILL BE LIBERATED FROM ITS BONDAGE TO DECAY AND BROUGHT INTO THE GLORIOUS FREEDOM OF THE CHILDREN OF GOD.

GENESIS 9:9-17; 2 PETER 3:5-7; ROMANS 8:21-23

THERE IS EVERY REASON TO BELIEVE THE REDEMPTION OF GOD'S CREATION TO BE COMPLETE ENOUGH TO ALSO INCLUDE ANIMALS LONG AGO EXTINCT.

GOD IS GOING TO RESURRECT HUMAN BEINGS WHO SUFFERED IN THE OLD WORLD- NOT MAKE NEW ONES.

THE LOGICAL CONCLUSION IS THAT GOD MAY ALSO RESURRECT SOME OF THE OLD ANIMALS FROM THE OLD EARTH.

ANIMALS WERE CREATED FOR GOD'S GLORY AND ALSO DISPLAY HIS GREATNESS SO WHY WOULD HE NOT HAVE THEM ANYMORE?

GOD DID NOT MAKE A MISTAKE WHEN HE MADE THE DINOSAURS OR ANY OTHER CREATURES. ALL CREATION SPEAKS OF HIS GLORY.

THERE IS NO REASON HE COULD NOT CREATE A TRUE JURASSIC PARK- BUT A PEACEFUL ONE- WHEN HE MAKES A NEW EARTH.

JOB 39-41

GOD CREATED ANIMALS WITH THEIR ENDEARING QUALITIES AND HAS USED THEM MANY TIMES TO TOUCH AND WARM OUR HEARTS.

THE BIBLE GIVES A JOYOUS MESSAGE THAT THE WHOLE CREATION (INCLUDING ANIMALS) WILL BE LIBERATED AND BE BROUGHT INTO THE GLORIOUS FREEDOM OF THE CHILDREN OF GOD.

ON THE NEW EARTH, AFTER MANKIND'S RESURRECTION, ANIMALS WHO ONCE SUFFERED WILL JOIN GOD'S CHILDREN IN A NEW AND PERFECT WORLD.

JESUS TELLS US THAT GOD IS BETTER THAN US AT GIVING GIFTS TO HIS CHILDREN.

IT CANNOT BE SAID FOR CERTAIN– BUT BASED ON MUCH SCRIPTURAL REFERENCE REGARDING ANIMALS IN HEAVEN, AS WELL AS GOD'S GENEROUS CHARACTER TO HIS CHILDREN– IT IS MOST LIKELY THAT THE FOLLOWER OF GOD CAN ALSO LOOK FORWARD TO A REUNION WITH ANIMALS AND PETS AS WELL!

BEHOLD, I AM MAKING *ALL* THINGS NEW.

ROMANS 8:21-23; MATTHEW 7:9-1; REVELATION 21:5

WHAT DOES THE BIBLE SAY ABOUT THE END OF THE WORLD?

SOME PEOPLE HAVE BEEN CONCERNED BECAUSE THEY THINK THE WORLD IS ENDING ON A CERTAIN DATE.

BUT THE MAYAN CALENDAR ENDS ON DECEMBER 21, 2012- THAT MUST BE THE END OF THE WORLD!

IN THE YEAR 999 PEOPLE THOUGHT THE WORLD WAS COMING TO AN END.

EVEN SOME PREACHERS HAVE SAID THAT JESUS CHRIST IS COMING BACK ON A SPECIFIC DAY, LIKE SEPTEMBER 11, 1988 OR MAY 21, 2011.

THE BIBLE DOES HAVE A LOT TO SAY ABOUT THE END TIMES- MANY BOOKS OF THE BIBLE DESCRIBE THE END OF THE WORLD- BUT THEY DON'T GIVE US THE EXACT DAY AND HOUR.

NO ONE KNOWS ABOUT THAT DAY OR HOUR, NOT EVEN THE ANGELS IN HEAVEN, NOR THE SON, BUT ONLY THE FATHER.

MATTHEW 24:36

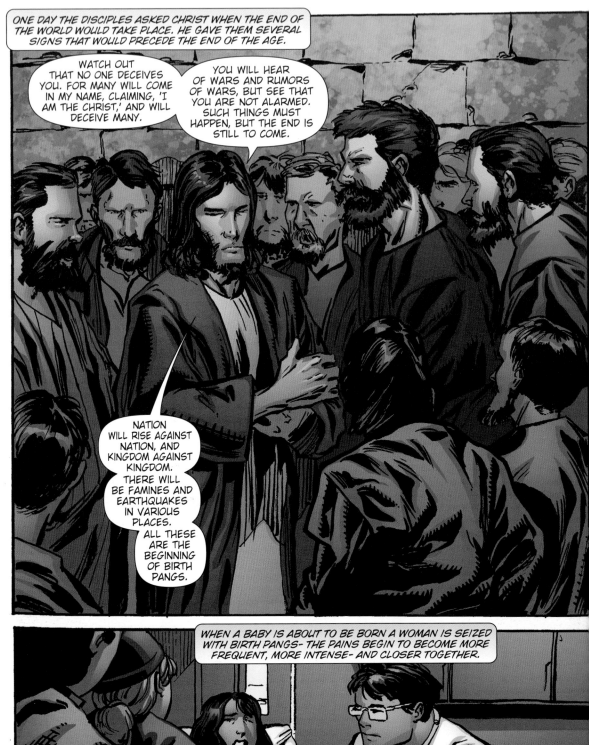

ONE DAY THE DISCIPLES ASKED CHRIST WHEN THE END OF THE WORLD WOULD TAKE PLACE. HE GAVE THEM SEVERAL SIGNS THAT WOULD PRECEDE THE END OF THE AGE.

WATCH OUT THAT NO ONE DECEIVES YOU. FOR MANY WILL COME IN MY NAME, CLAIMING, 'I AM THE CHRIST,' AND WILL DECEIVE MANY.

YOU WILL HEAR OF WARS AND RUMORS OF WARS, BUT SEE THAT YOU ARE NOT ALARMED. SUCH THINGS MUST HAPPEN, BUT THE END IS STILL TO COME.

NATION WILL RISE AGAINST NATION, AND KINGDOM AGAINST KINGDOM. THERE WILL BE FAMINES AND EARTHQUAKES IN VARIOUS PLACES. ALL THESE ARE THE BEGINNING OF BIRTH PANGS.

WHEN A BABY IS ABOUT TO BE BORN A WOMAN IS SEIZED WITH BIRTH PANGS- THE PAINS BEGIN TO BECOME MORE FREQUENT, MORE INTENSE- AND CLOSER TOGETHER.

FALSE MESSIAHS, WARFARE, FAMINES AND EARTHQUAKES HAVE BEEN PRESENT SINCE THE BEGINNING OF THE WORLD- BUT NOW THEY HAVE BECOME MORE FREQUENT AND MORE INTENSE.

MATTHEW 24:5-8

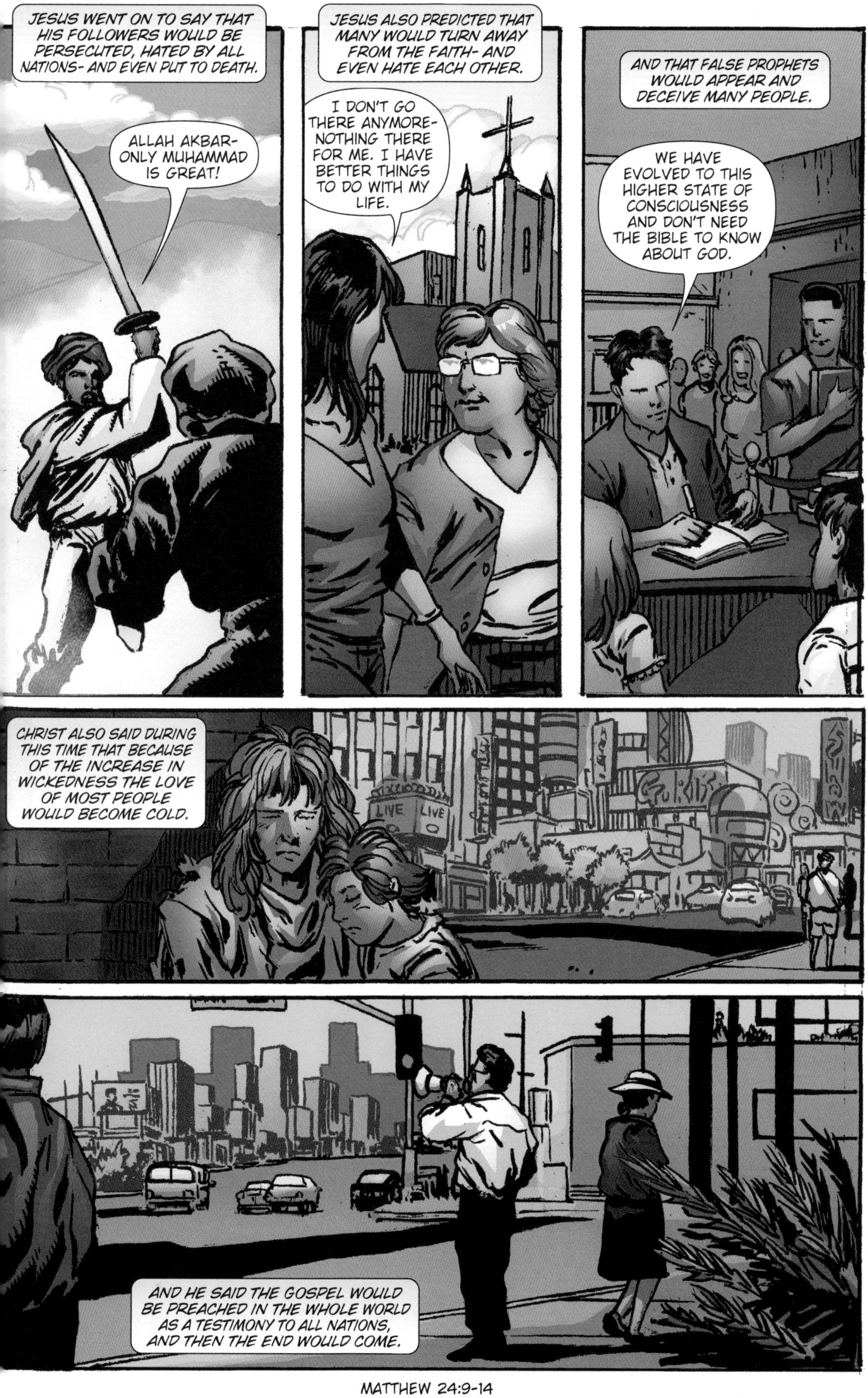
JESUS WENT ON TO SAY THAT HIS FOLLOWERS WOULD BE PERSECUTED, HATED BY ALL NATIONS- AND EVEN PUT TO DEATH.
ALLAH AKBAR- ONLY MUHAMMAD IS GREAT!
JESUS ALSO PREDICTED THAT MANY WOULD TURN AWAY FROM THE FAITH- AND EVEN HATE EACH OTHER.
I DON'T GO THERE ANYMORE- NOTHING THERE FOR ME. I HAVE BETTER THINGS TO DO WITH MY LIFE.
AND THAT FALSE PROPHETS WOULD APPEAR AND DECEIVE MANY PEOPLE.
WE HAVE EVOLVED TO THIS HIGHER STATE OF CONSCIOUSNESS AND DON'T NEED THE BIBLE TO KNOW ABOUT GOD.
CHRIST ALSO SAID DURING THIS TIME THAT BECAUSE OF THE INCREASE IN WICKEDNESS THE LOVE OF MOST PEOPLE WOULD BECOME COLD.
LIVE
LIVE
AND HE SAID THE GOSPEL WOULD BE PREACHED IN THE WHOLE WORLD AS A TESTIMONY TO ALL NATIONS, AND THEN THE END WOULD COME.

MATTHEW 24:9-14

THE APOSTLE PAUL IN HIS LETTERS ALSO WARNED THAT THE LAST DAYS WOULD SEE AN INCREASE IN FALSE TEACHING, WITH PEOPLE ABANDONING THE FAITH AND "FOLLOWING DECEIVING SPIRITS AND THINGS TAUGHT BY DEMONS."

OTHER POSSIBLE SIGNS INCLUDE THE REBUILDING OF THE TEMPLE IN JERUSALEM, MORE HOSTILITY TOWARDS THE NATION OF ISRAEL, AND A MOVEMENT TO A ONE WORLD GOVERNMENT.

ONE OF THE MOST PROMINENT SIGNS OF THE END TIMES IS THE RE-ESTABLISHMENT OF THE NATION OF ISRAEL- NUMEROUS PROPHETS HAD FORETOLD THAT GOD WOULD BRING THE JEWS BACK TO ISRAEL.

IN 1948, ISRAEL WAS RECOGNIZED AS A SOVEREIGN STATE- OFFICIALLY FOR THE FIRST TIME SINCE A.D. 70.

I TIMOTHY 4:1; II TIMOTHY 3:19; II THESSALONIANS 2:3; GENESIS 17:8; EZEKIEL 37; DANIEL 10:14

GOD WANTS PEOPLE TO BE WISE AND DISCERNING AND NOT INTERPRET ANY OF THESE AS THE IMMEDIATE ARRIVAL OF THE END TIMES.

HE GAVE US INFORMATION IN THE BIBLE SO THAT WE CAN BE PREPARED.

SOME BELIEVE THE BIBLE TEACHES THAT CHRIST WILL COME TO TAKE HIS FOLLOWERS FROM THE EARTH BEFORE THIS NEXT MAJOR EVENT.

WE DON'T KNOW THAT FOR CERTAIN— BUT WE DO KNOW THAT GOD WILL EITHER DELIVER HIS PEOPLE OR BE WITH THEM IN A SPECIAL WAY THROUGH THE TOUGH TIMES THAT COME ON THE EARTH.

AROUND THIS SAME TIME PERIOD A RULER WILL ARISE THAT THE BIBLE TERMS 'THE ANTICHRIST.'

AT FIRST HE WILL BE FRIENDLY WITH ISRAEL AND WILL SIGN A PEACE AGREEMENT WITH ISRAEL FOR SEVEN YEARS.

THIS WILL BE A TIME OF TERRIBLE WARS, FAMINES, PLAGUES AND NATURAL DISASTERS.

I THESSALONIANS 4;13-18; I CORINTHIANS 15:51-54; DANIEL 9:27; REVELATION 6-19

HALFWAY INTO THE SEVEN YEAR PERIOD THE ANTICHRIST WILL BREAK HIS PEACE AGREEMENT WITH ISRAEL AND TURN ON THE JEWS.

HE WILL ALSO SET HIMSELF UP IN THE TEMPLE TO BE WORSHIPPED.

HORRIBLE PLAGUES, MONSTROUS EARTHQUAKES AND FAMINES WILL RAVAGE THE EARTH.

THIS WORLD LEADER WILL LAUNCH A FINAL ATTACK AGAINST JERUSALEM THAT DRAWS IN ARMIES FROM ALL OVER THE WORLD.

AT SOME POINT IN THIS VICIOUS BATTLE, JESUS CHRIST RETURNS TO DESTROY THIS ANTICHRIST. THE ANTICHRIST AND THE FALSE PROPHET WITH HIM ARE THROWN ALIVE INTO THE FIERY LAKE OF BURNING SULPHUR.

DANIEL 9:27; II THESSALONIANS 2:3-10; REVELATION 19:11-21

THEN FOR 1,000 YEARS SATAN IS BOUND WITH A CHAIN AND JESUS CHRIST RULES THE WORLD FROM JERUSALEM.

IT IS A TIME OF PEACE AND PROSPERITY LIKE THE WORLD HAS NEVER KNOWN.

AFTER THE 1,000 YEARS IS ENDED SATAN IS RELEASED ONE LAST TIME. HE DECEIVES A NUMBER OF MEN AND WOMEN- AND INCITES THIS ARMY TO INVADE JERUSALEM WHERE CHRIST IS REIGNING.

BUT FIRE COMES DOWN FROM HEAVEN AND DESTROYS THIS LAST REBELLIOUS ARMY AND SATAN IS THROWN INTO THE LAKE OF FIRE.

THEN THE DEAD ALL OVER THE WORLD ARE RAISED TO LIFE AND EVERY SINGLE MAN AND WOMAN IS JUDGED BEFORE THE GREAT WHITE THRONE OF CHRIST.

AT THIS JUDGMENT SEAT OF CHRIST, HIS FOLLOWERS WILL BE REWARDED FOR GOOD WORKS AND FAITHFUL SERVICE DURING THEIR TIME ON EARTH.

SOME CHRISTIANS WILL LOSE REWARDS- BUT NOT ETERNAL LIFE- FOR LACK OF SERVICE AND OBEDIENCE.

CHRIST THEN JUDGES ALL THOSE WHO HAVE REFUSED HIM AND HIS FORGIVENESS- THEIR AWFUL FATE IS TO BE CAST INTO THE LAKE OF FIRE- FOREVER.

I CORINTHIANS 3:11-15; II CORINTHIANS 5:10; REVELATION 20:1-15

THE EVENT THAT HAPPENS NEXT IS WHAT PEOPLE USUALLY MEAN WHEN THEY REFER TO THE "END OF THE WORLD."

THE APOSTLE PETER WROTE THAT THE FIRST HEAVENS AND THE FIRST EARTH WOULD ONE DAY BE DESTROYED BY FIRE.

THE EVENT WILL BE CATACLYSMIC- AND LOUD.

STARS AND GALAXIES WILL BE CONSUMED IN A TREMENDOUS EXPLOSION AND THE EARTH WILL BE LAID BARE.

PETER THEN ADDS- SINCE EVERYTHING WILL BE DESTROYED IN THIS WAY, WHAT KIND OF PEOPLE OUGHT YOU TO BE?

YOU OUGHT TO LIVE HOLY AND GODLY LIVES AS YOU LOOK FORWARD TO THE DAY OF GOD AND SPEED ITS COMING.

THE APOSTLE IS SAYING WE SHOULD LIVE OUR LIVES IN SUCH A WAY THAT REFLECTS OUR UNDERSTANDING OF WHAT IS GOING TO HAPPEN IN THE FUTURE.

OUR LIVES SHOULD BE A TESTIMONY TO THOSE WHO DO NOT KNOW CHRIST, AND WE SHOULD BE TELLING OTHERS ABOUT HIM SO THEY CAN ESCAPE THE TERRIBLE FATE THAT AWAITS THOSE WHO REJECT HIM.

II PETER 3:10-13